My Magical Friends

Baby Phoenix Makes Friends

by Jessica Lee Anderson
illustrated by Wendy Tan

SCHOLASTIC INC.

For Ava and Emily and their magical friendship.
—J.L.A.

To my family, who have always been my biggest cheerleaders.
—Wendy Tan Shiau Wei

ISBN 978-1-339-02639-8

10 9 8 7 6 5 4 3 2 1   24 25 26 27 28

Printed in China   68
First edition 2024
Original book design by Joan Moloney

Best friends Shelby and Isabella dressed up
as princesses in Shelby's playroom.
"You look so pretty in your crown," Isabella said.
"You too, Isabella!" Shelby said.
The girls jumped when they heard a knock
on the front door.
"Lucas is here!" Shelby's mom called.
The best friends looked at each other in surprise.

Lucas was Shelby's neighbor. He hardly ever talked to them.

Isabella and Shelby ran to answer the door. Lucas stared at their crowns. "You both look like princesses," he said.

Shelby and Isabella giggled. "Thank you," they said at the same time.

Lucas frowned.

"Is everything okay?" Isabella asked.

"My birthday party is today, but no one can make it," Lucas said.
"We would love to be your guests!" Shelby said.
Isabella nodded in agreement.
Lucas went home to prepare.
The girls had some time to play before Lucas's birthday party.

Shelby and Isabella loved Shelby's play set with the castles, tiny houses, and forest.

"Let's add to the fun!" Shelby exclaimed, holding a small gold box.

"The magic bracelet!" Isabella said.

Whenever Shelby wore it, the girls traveled to a magic kingdom.

They loved meeting new magical friends there.

The bracelet glowed when Shelby put it on.
Isabella and Shelby grabbed hands and looked
at the bracelet.
They felt a funny tug and a tingle.
A bright light flashed.

Shelby and Isabella blinked and looked around. They were not in Shelby's playroom anymore. The friends stood on the beach near the castle. "Your magical bracelet is amazing!" exclaimed Isabella.

"Look!" Shelby said, pointing at mermaids swimming. The girls watched in wonder as one flipped in the air. Then they saw something splashing in the water. "Help!" a voice cried.

Isabella and Shelby helped bring a baby phoenix to the shore.
He had beautiful wings and a long tail.
"Are you all right?" Isabella asked.

"Yes, I'm okay. Thank you, Princesses," the baby phoenix said. "I'm Elio."

The girls smiled at each other. Magical creatures often thought they were real princesses.

"I'm Princess Isabella and that's Princess Shelby," Isabella said, winking at her friend.

Elio shook his feathers to dry off. Elio's feathers now sparkled and glowed.

"What happened, Elio?" Isabella asked.
"I'm the only phoenix in the enchanted kingdom.
It gets lonely. I wanted to become friends and play
with the mermaids, but the water was too deep
for me," Elio said.

"When you feel lonely, it's good to reach out to others," Isabella said.

"Yes, and we know you will make some friends, Elio," Shelby said.

"Friends can help you feel less alone," Isabella added, wrapping an arm around Shelby.

Just then, some unicorns ran by, kicking a ball to one another on the beach.

"I'll try again to make new friends. If I act like a unicorn, they will want to be friends!" Elio said.

The girls watched as Elio joined the unicorn game.
Elio tried to neigh like the unicorns.
He missed the ball when the unicorns passed
it to him.
Elio tried to gallop to keep up with the unicorns.

"You're full of energy! Keep trying,"
a unicorn said.
Elio wobbled as he tripped over his wings.
"You got this!" said another unicorn.

The girls raced to keep up.
"You can do it!" Shelby shouted.
Suddenly, Isabella tripped over a piece of driftwood at the same time Elio tripped over his wings again.

"Oh no!" Shelby said.

Shelby helped Isabella get up. "Are you okay?" she asked.

"I scraped my hand, but I'm fine," Isabella said.

Elio flew back to the girls with tears in his eyes.
"What's wrong, Elio? Are you okay?" Shelby
asked.
"I'm okay, but I could not keep up with the
unicorns. What if they don't want to be friends
with me?" Elio said with more tears.

Isabella reached out to comfort Elio.
"Oh no, you're hurt, Princess Isabella!" Elio cried.

The unicorns stopped playing and the mermaids
stopped swimming.
They came closer to see what was wrong.

Elio took Isabella's hand into his wing.
He held her hand up to his face, nuzzling it.
A tear dropped onto Isabella's skin.

"Your scrape is healed, Isabella!" Shelby exclaimed. The girls looked in awe at Isabella's magically healed hand.

"It feels much better," Isabella said.

"Thank you, Elio!"

"That's what friends are for!" said Elio.

"You may not swim like a mermaid or play like a unicorn, but you're a wonderful phoenix," Shelby said.

"You don't have to change who you are to make friends, Elio. You made new friends by being yourself," Isabella said.

"You are fun, loving, and one of a kind,"
Shelby added.

The mermaids and unicorns nodded in agreement.

Elio flew up in the air with delight.

The unicorns and the mermaids cheered.

Elio looked around and smiled. "You're right, Princesses. I *don't* need to change myself to make friends. I'm a one-of-a-kind phoenix and my new friends like me as I am!" he said. The magical creatures cheered again! Elio sang a happy tune.

Isabella and Shelby gave Elio a hug.

"Do you want to play a game?" Elio asked.

"We want to, but there's a boy who is feeling alone we want to help, too," Shelby said.

"You are very kind princesses," Elio said.

The girls walked to the castle.

Elio flew above them singing another happy tune.

At the castle, Elio waved good-bye to the girls.

"Good-bye, Elio," the girls said.

As Elio flew back to the beach, Shelby and Isabella held hands.
They looked at the magic bracelet.
When the bracelet glowed, they felt a funny tug and a tingle.
A bright light flashed.

Just like that, they were back in Shelby's playroom.
Shelby looked at her bracelet again.

"Isabella, look at this pretty phoenix charm!"
Shelby said.

"It's one of a kind," Isabella said, smiling.

When Isabella reached into her pocket, she found not one but two phoenix feathers!

"Magical," Shelby said.

"I'm going to give the extra feather to Lucas at his birthday party," Isabella said.

"We better get ready for more fun!" Shelby said.

The girls had a wonderful afternoon with their new friend Lucas!